In Her Shoes
ISBN 978-1-7332980-6-3

Parents communicate by speaking, but kids learn by watching.
Always remember that your actions are
heard before your voice is understood.

Stephanie is holding Ava on her chest for the first time. The waves of emotions are washing over her while she thinks about the fact that she is officially a mom now.

As Ava feeds from Stephanie, the special bond between mother and daughter is being established.

Stephanie is smiling at Ava while she is changing her. She is thinking about the precious life that she is going to help mold. Ava is smiling back at her mom because she is happy that her diaper is being changed.

While Stephanie is getting dressed Ava is trying to stick her foot in her mom's shoe. Stephanie smiles at the sight and thinks that one day she will be in her shoes with her own family.

Ava sees her mom dancing to music while putting on makeup. She laughs and enjoys the fun time with her mom.

Stephanie is cooking a meal and Ava is there to help. Stephanie is happy to see that Ava is following her lead and tries to learn new things.

Ava sees her parents, Stephanie and Dameon, laying on the couch watching tv. She always smiles at the sight of their happiness and knows that she wants that for herself.

Ava tells her mom that she thinks that she has a crush on a boy. Stephanie tells her that she will always be there to listen to her and help guide her through her growing emotions.

Ava goes out on her first date and remembers the conversations with her mom where she was told to always value herself and be safe.

Ava is graduating from high school and is excited about starting the new phase of her life in college. Her mom is extremely proud of the young woman that she is becoming.

Ava is in college and starts to feel overwhelmed with the amount of work that she has to do. She then remembers how hard her mom worked and wants to make sure that she does not let her down.

Ava is graduating from college and her family is excited to see her conquer another phase in her life. She is happy to see the proud look on her mom's face.

Ava is working hard in her new job. She is striving to move up in her career.

Ava has been doing great in her career and just received a promotion. She is overjoyed and called her mom to tell her the great news. Stephanie is happy to hear that Ava's hard work is paying off.

Ava calls her mom to tell her that she is engaged. Stephanie congratulates her and smiles while knowing that Ava has used her teachings to find love.

Ava is now pregnant and is rubbing her belly. She is thinking about the life that is growing in her and how that will change her life. She is experiencing love on a level that she has never felt before.

Ava has just given birth to her daughter Denise. Denise is laying on Ava's chest asleep and Ava is looking at her with total amazement and excitement because her child is now here.

Ava and Denise are home now. Denise is laying in her play area while Ava is watching her play. Denise has brought a new sense of purpose to Ava's life.

Ava is holding Denise while thinking about her life. She is recalling the various conversations and lessons that her mom taught her and she is hoping to be as great of a mom to Denise that her mom was to her.

Denise is standing by Ava's leg while looking up at her. Ava catches her daughter smiling at her. Ava realizes that her daughter has put her in the same shoes that her mom wore while she raised her.

Made in the USA
Middletown, DE
29 July 2020